CLASSIC LITERATURE

Essential Literary Genres

BY VALERIE BODDEN

Essential Library

An Imprint of Abdo Publishing | abdopublishing.com

ABDOPUBLISHING.COM

Published by Abdo Publishing, a division of ABDO, PO Box 398166, Minneapolis, Minnesota 55439.

Printed in the United States of America, North Mankato, Minnesota
092016
012017

THIS BOOK CONTAINS RECYCLED MATERIALS

Interior Photos: Johnson Wilson & Co./Library of Congress, 10–11; Universal Studios/Photofest, 12, 15, 16, 21, 23, 30; Everett Historical/Shutterstock Images, 35; Twentieth Century Fox Film Corporation/Photofest, 36, 39, 41, 43; Eric Charbonneau/Invision for Twentieth Century Fox/AP Images, 44–45; Phil Bray/Buena Vista Pictures/Photofest, 54–55, 57, 59, 61; @Parisa/Splash News/Newscom, 64–65; Shane Sato/Buena Vista Pictures/Photofest, 71; AP Images, 77; Panya Piyaprakongsri/Shutterstock Images, 79; Cinecom/Photofest, 85; MGM Home Entertainment/Photofest, 87; Pascal Saez/Writer Pictures/AP Images, 91

Editor: Jenna Gleisner
Series Designer: Maggie Villaume

PUBLISHER'S CATALOGING-IN-PUBLICATION DATA

Names: Bodden, Valerie, author.
Title: Classic literature / by Valerie Bodden.
Description: Minneapolis, MN : Abdo Publishing, 2017. | Series: Essential literary genres | Includes bibliographical references and index.
Identifiers: LCCN 2016945203 | ISBN 9781680783773 (lib. bdg.) | ISBN 9781680797305 (ebook)
Subjects: LCSH: Literature--Juvenile literature. | Literary form--Juvenile literature.
Classification: DDC 809--dc23
LC record available at http://lccn.loc.gov/2016945203

CONTENTS

1

INTRODUCTION TO LITERARY GENRES

Why do we read and write literature? Telling stories is an integral part of being human, a universal experience across history and cultures. Literature as we know it today is the written form of these stories and ideas. Writing allows authors to take their readers on a journey that crosses the boundaries of space and time. Literature allows us to understand the experiences of others and express experiences of our own.

What Is a Genre?

A genre is a specific category, or type, of literature. Broad genres of literature include nonfiction, poetry, drama, and fiction. Smaller groupings include subject-based genres such as mystery, science fiction, romance, or fantasy. Literature can also be classified by its audience, such as young adult (YA) or children's, or its format, such as a graphic novel or picture book.

What Are Literary Theory and Criticism?

Literary theory gives us tools to help decode a text. On one level, we can examine the words and phrases the author uses so we can interpret or debate his or her message. We can ask questions about how the book's structure creates an effect on the reader, and whether this is the effect the author intended. We can analyze symbolism or themes in a work. We can dive deeper by asking how a work either supports or challenges society and its values or traditions.

You can look at these questions using different criticisms, or schools of thought. Each type of criticism asks you to look at the work from a different perspective. Perhaps you want to examine what the work says about the writer's life or the time period in which the work was created. Biographical or historical criticism considers these questions. Or perhaps you are interested in what the work says about the role of women or the structure of society. Feminist or Marxist theories seek to answer those types of questions.

How Do You Apply Literary Criticism?

You write an analysis when you use a literary or critical approach to examine and question a work. The theory you choose is a lens through which you can view the work, or a springboard for asking questions about the work. Applying a theory helps you think critically. You are free to question the work and make an assertion about it. If you choose to examine a work using racial criticism, for example, you may ask questions about how the work challenges or upholds racial structures in society. Or you may ask how a character's race affects his or her identity or development throughout the work.

Forming a Thesis

Form your questions and find answers in the work or other related materials. Then you can create a thesis. The thesis is the key point in your analysis. It is your argument about the work based on the school of thought you are using. For example, if you want to approach a work using feminist criticism, you could write the following thesis: The character of Margy in Sissy Johnson's *Margy Sings the Blues* uses her songwriting to subvert traditional gender roles.

HOW TO MAKE A THESIS STATEMENT

In an analysis, a thesis statement typically appears at the end of the introductory paragraph. It is usually only one sentence long and states the author's main idea.

Providing Evidence

Once you have formed a thesis, you must provide evidence to support it. Evidence will usually take the form of examples and quotations from the work itself, often including dialogue from a character. You may wish to address what others have written about the work. Quotes from these individuals may help support your claim. If you find any quotes or examples that contradict your thesis, you will need to create an argument against them. For instance: Many critics claim Margy's actions uphold traditional gender roles, even if her songs went against them. However, the novel's resolution proves Margy had the power to change society through her music.

HOW TO SUPPORT A THESIS STATEMENT

An analysis should include several arguments that support the thesis's claim. An argument is one or two sentences long and is supported by evidence from the work being discussed. Organize the arguments into paragraphs. These paragraphs make up the body of the analysis.

Concluding the Essay

After you have written several arguments and included evidence to support them, finish the essay with a conclusion. The conclusion restates the ideas from the

HOW TO CONCLUDE AN ESSAY

Begin your conclusion with a recap of the thesis and a brief summary of the most important or strongest arguments. Leave readers with a final thought that puts the essay in a larger context or considers its wider implications.

thesis and summarizes some of the main points from the essay. The conclusion's final thought often considers additional implications for the essay or gives the reader something to ponder further.

In This Book

In this book, you will read summaries of works, each followed by an analysis. Critical thinking sections will give you a chance to consider other theses and questions about the work. Did you agree with the author's analysis? What other questions are raised by the thesis and its arguments? You can also see other directions the author could have pursued to analyze the work. Then, in the Analyze It section in the final pages of this book, you will have an opportunity to create your own analysis paper.

Classic Literature

The book you are reading focuses on classic literature. There is no one agreed-on definition of what makes a work of literature a classic. Most scholars agree that works of classic literature have artistic merit in some form—through either the beauty of their language or the truths they express. Classics usually focus on universal themes, such as beauty and truth or love and hate.

In addition, most classics have stood the test of time. These are novels that were published decades—or even centuries—ago, but continue to be recognized as important. Often, they are a reflection of the time in which they were written. Although newer books are rarely considered classics in the traditional sense, they can be recognized as modern classics. These are books of significant artistry and importance that haven't yet stood the test of time but are likely to endure.

LOOK FOR THE GUIDES

Throughout the chapters that analyze the works, thesis statements have been highlighted. The box next to the thesis helps explain what questions are being raised about the work. Supporting arguments have also been highlighted. The boxes next to the arguments help explain how these points support the thesis. The conclusions are also accompanied by explanatory boxes. Look for these guides throughout each analysis.

2

AN OVERVIEW OF *PRIDE AND PREJUDICE*

First published in 1813, Jane Austen's *Pride and Prejudice* received little notice at the time. The novel is now recognized as one of the greats of classic literature. Set during the Regency period of early nineteenth-century England, the novel relates the story of Elizabeth Bennet, the second of five sisters born to a gentleman and his wife.

The novel opens as Elizabeth's mother, Mrs. Bennet, tells her family that Netherfield, a nearby estate, has been leased by a wealthy young man named Mr. Bingley. Immediately, Mrs. Bennet sets her eyes on marrying off one of her girls to him.

Jane Austen published *Pride and Prejudice* anonymously.

Finding husbands for her daughters remains her chief concern throughout the book, since the family's estate, Longbourn, has been entailed, meaning that since Mr. Bennet has no sons, the estate will pass to his cousin, Mr. Collins, after his death.

Within days of Mr. Bingley's arrival, Elizabeth and her sisters meet him at a ball. With him are his sisters, Miss Bingley and Mrs. Hurst, as well as a friend, Mr. Darcy. Bingley is friendly and dances with many of the young ladies, giving special attention to Elizabeth's older sister, Jane. But Darcy watches everyone coldly from the sidelines.

Mrs. Bennet, *left*, is solely concerned with marrying off her five daughters.

An Illness

Jane is soon invited to dine with Miss Bingley and Mrs. Hurst at Netherfield. Her mother refuses to allow Jane to use the carriage, insisting that she instead travel by horseback so that if it rains she won't be able to return home. It does rain, and Jane falls ill as a result, requiring her to remain at Netherfield. Worried about her sister, Elizabeth walks the three miles (4.8 km) to Netherfield through muddy fields to visit her. Later that day, Miss Bingley remarks to Darcy and Bingley how wild and messy Elizabeth looked. She also points out that one of Elizabeth and Jane's uncles is in trade in the Cheapside district of London. The other is an attorney, meaning he is not a gentleman but works for a living. Darcy says their inferior relatives will lessen the girls' ability to attract a husband of wealth and status.

Elizabeth spends her days at Netherfield taking care of Jane. After several days, Jane is finally well enough to go home, and Elizabeth is grateful to leave Netherfield.

Meeting Mr. Collins and Mr. Wickham

Soon afterward, Mr. Collins visits Longbourn. Elizabeth finds him odd with his overly formal language and his constant references to his patroness, Lady Catherine de Bourgh, who secured him a living, or a church and parsonage where he could live and work. The girls take Mr. Collins for a walk to Meryton, the nearby village where the militia is stationed, much to the joy of Elizabeth's impulsive, boy-crazy younger sister Lydia. With her wild, outgoing behavior, Lydia is already a favorite of many of the officers. In Meryton, the girls meet a new member of the militia, Mr. Wickham.

A short time later, Elizabeth talks with Wickham at a party. He tells her his father was the steward of Darcy's father. He says the elder Mr. Darcy's will specified that the next living to become available should be given to Wickham. But when the living became available, Darcy refused to give it to Wickham, leaving him in poverty. Elizabeth is shocked and feels great pity for Wickham—and deep anger toward Darcy. When she later relates the story to Jane, Jane is unwilling to believe either man could have been at fault.

The next week, a ball is held at Netherfield. Elizabeth dresses carefully, looking forward to dancing with Wickham, but when she arrives, she finds he is absent. His friend tells her Wickham wanted to avoid meeting Darcy. After being forced to dance the first two numbers with Mr. Collins, who has been showing

Although she is angry with Darcy, Elizabeth accepts the dance because she can think of no way to decline.

her particular attention, Elizabeth is asked to dance by Darcy. Meanwhile, Jane enjoys the evening with Bingley, with whom she is quickly falling in love.

A Proposal

The day after the ball, Mr. Collins proposes marriage to Elizabeth. She refuses him, despite her mother's insistence she accept. Afterward, Elizabeth's friend Charlotte offers to keep Mr. Collins occupied in secret hopes of securing him for herself. Within days, Mr. Collins proposes to Charlotte, and she accepts. Elizabeth is shocked that her friend would agree to marry such an insensible, ridiculous man.

Even though marrying Mr. Collins would ensure economic stability, Elizabeth refuses because she does not love, or even like, him.

Meanwhile, Jane receives word from Miss Bingley that the group from Netherfield has abruptly left for London. The letter further implies Mr. Bingley will marry Miss Darcy, Mr. Darcy's sister. Elizabeth is convinced Miss Bingley is scheming to keep Bingley from Jane, but Jane refuses to believe it.

As for her own affairs, although Elizabeth has spent considerable time with Wickham, he turns his attentions to a young woman who has inherited a fortune. Although slightly disappointed, Elizabeth realizes she had "never been much in love" with him.[1]

Another Proposal

As spring approaches, Elizabeth visits Charlotte in her new home with Mr. Collins. She learns Charlotte has arranged her days so that she spends little time with her husband. While staying at the parsonage, Elizabeth joins Charlotte and Mr. Collins in visiting Lady Catherine's estate, Rosings, several times.

Two weeks into the visit, Lady Catherine's nephews, Mr. Darcy and his cousin, Colonel Fitzwilliam, join the group. One day, Colonel Fitzwilliam mentions to Elizabeth that Darcy has recently saved a friend—possibly Bingley—from "the inconveniences of a most imprudent marriage."[2] Elizabeth realizes this is why Bingley stopped courting Jane. That night she fakes a headache and does not go to Rosings with the others.

While Elizabeth is at the parsonage alone, Darcy visits and shocks her by declaring his love for her. He says he has tried to convince himself not to propose because of her family's inferior social status and imprudent behavior. Insulted, Elizabeth refuses the proposal, calling him ungentlemanly. She accuses him of ruining the happiness of her sister and treating Mr. Wickham unfairly.

Change of Heart

The next day, Darcy gives Elizabeth a letter. In it, he explains that he convinced Bingley to leave Netherfield not only because of the inferiority of Jane's family but also because he believed her indifferent to Bingley. He also relates what really happened with Wickham. The elder Mr. Darcy's will had specified that Wickham was to receive a living only if he became a clergyman. But a few months after the elder Mr. Darcy's death, Wickham had told Darcy he didn't intend to enter the clergy. Darcy gave him financial compensation in place of the living. That seemed to be the end of their relationship, until Wickham attempted to elope with Miss Darcy, who was then only 15. The scheme was broken up by an unexpected visit from Darcy; if it hadn't been, Wickham would have gotten Miss Darcy's sizable fortune.

After reading the letter, Elizabeth is ashamed of her own behavior toward Darcy. She walks to clear her head, and when she returns, she learns Darcy and Colonel Fitzwilliam have left Rosings. A few days later, Elizabeth leaves as scheduled.

At home, Elizabeth rejoices to learn the militia—and Wickham—will soon be leaving Meryton. Her youngest sister, Lydia, has been invited to accompany them. Elizabeth fears Lydia will expose the entire family to ridicule or worse with her inappropriate behavior.

Pemberley

Meanwhile, Elizabeth takes a trip with her aunt and uncle, Mr. and Mrs. Gardiner, to Derbyshire, where her aunt grew up. Derbyshire also happens to be the location of Pemberley, Darcy's great estate. The Gardiners convince Elizabeth to take a tour of Pemberley, since they have learned Darcy is not home.

As they tour the grounds, Darcy unexpectedly returns. Both Elizabeth and Darcy are shocked to see each other, but Darcy asks Elizabeth to introduce her friends to him. She does so and is surprised at how friendly he acts toward her aunt and uncle—some of her inferior relatives he had spoken against in his proposal. As she spends more time with him at Pemberley, she is amazed by the change in his manners, which have become much less proud and more open.

Scandal

The next day, Elizabeth receives news from Jane that Lydia and Wickham have run off together. They apparently haven't eloped—and although an elopement would have caused a scandal, the fact that they are living together without being married is even worse and will bring disgrace to the whole family.

As a distressed Elizabeth is about to leave to find her aunt and uncle, she runs into Darcy. She bursts into tears and tells him everything. He listens and then paces in silence. Elizabeth assumes it is because he wants nothing more to do with her or her family. Although she doesn't blame him, she realizes she loves him.

The Gardiners take Elizabeth back to Longbourn, where they find that Mr. Bennet has gone to London to try to find Lydia and Wickham. Mr. Gardiner leaves for London to help, and after a few days, Mr. Bennet returns home. Two days later, the family receives a letter from Mr. Gardiner, saying Lydia and Wickham have been found and will be married. Although everyone rejoices, Mr. Bennet says Mr. Gardiner likely had to pay Wickham 10,000 pounds to secure the marriage.

After Lydia's wedding, Elizabeth learns from her Aunt Gardiner that Darcy was the one who found Lydia and Wickham and paid Wickham off. But he insisted on making the Gardiners take credit for everything.

Happily Ever After

Mr. Bingley and Mr. Darcy return to Netherfield. Darcy soon leaves for London on business, and Bingley proposes to Jane. A week later, Lady Catherine arrives at Longbourn. She orders Elizabeth to promise never to marry her nephew. Elizabeth refuses, saying she won't consider Lady Catherine when deciding what to do with her own life.

Soon afterward, Darcy returns and confesses he still loves Elizabeth. Her feelings toward him have changed since his last proposal, and this time she accepts. Elizabeth and Jane are married on the same day. Jane and Bingley move near Pemberley. The sisters are happily married and enjoy seeing each other frequently.

At the end of the novel, Jane and Bingley are happily married.

3

ELIZABETH BENNET AS A STRONG WOMAN

Classic literature is often a reflection of its time period, and this is especially true in the way it portrays the roles of men and women in society. Feminist criticism looks at the types of roles female characters are assigned in a work. Are women presented as strong and intelligent, making their own decisions, or do they seem helpless and weak?

At its core, the plot of *Pride and Prejudice* revolves around a group of young women and their need to find husbands. This was no small matter in Austen's day, when marrying was often the only way a woman of upper-class England had to ensure she would be provided for. Yet Austen's novel goes deeper than simply

Elizabeth Bennet is a strong female character who benefits from going against society's expectations.

THESIS STATEMENT

The thesis statement lays out the point of the essay: "*Pride and Prejudice* criticizes women's roles in early nineteenth-century England by using minor female characters as foils to show Elizabeth as a strong woman meant to be admired for not blindly accepting society's expectations."

ARGUMENT ONE

The first argument explores marriage and women's roles in the novel: "Because of their limited position in society, the women in *Pride and Prejudice* are preoccupied with marriage."

relaying a series of husband hunts. *Pride and Prejudice* criticizes women's roles in early nineteenth-century England by using minor female characters as foils to show Elizabeth as a strong woman meant to be admired for not blindly accepting society's expectations.

Because of their limited position in society, the women in *Pride and Prejudice* are preoccupied with marriage. The novel illustrates this in its opening line: "It is a truth universally acknowledged, that a single man in possession of a good fortune, must be in want of a wife."[1] This ironic statement actually means the opposite: women are always after a single man of large fortune. In the society of the time, females generally inherited little, if anything, from their fathers. Marriage was viewed as "the only honourable provision for well-educated young women of small fortune."[2] Even if a woman was well-educated, she could do nothing to earn money with her learning. Instead, she was expected to make a career of being a wife. In addition, well-educated did not necessarily mean a young girl attended school. Instead, she was often taught only what she needed to know to run a household, along with perhaps some socially acceptable skills, such as drawing or music.

The novel's minor female characters illustrate varying reactions to these limited roles. Mrs. Bennet, whose greatest desire is to see her daughters married, seizes on the idea of one of them marrying Mr. Bingley before they have even met him. It matters little to her what the man is like. She cares only that he is "a single man of large fortune."[3] Mrs. Bennet's desire to marry her daughters off is so great that she is willing to sacrifice their happiness—and even their health. She is so determined to throw Jane at Bingley that she sends her to Netherfield on horseback even though it is likely to rain. And she demands that Elizabeth marry Mr. Collins, even though Elizabeth would be miserable.

ARGUMENT TWO

The next argument looks at how various female characters respond to society's restrictions: "The novel's minor female characters illustrate varying reactions to these limited roles."

Jane, on the other hand, is all innocence. When Elizabeth tells her of the dispute between Wickham and Darcy, Jane defends both, saying there must have been some sort of misunderstanding. She also refuses to believe Miss Bingley would willfully deceive her about Bingley's intentions to marry Miss Darcy because doing so would mean Miss Bingley was "acting unnaturally and wrong"—something Jane cannot fathom.[4]

In contrast to Jane's innocent nature is Charlotte's rational, calculating attitude toward marriage. Charlotte has no feelings for Mr. Collins—and in fact finds him "irksome"—yet she accepts his proposal anyway.[5] She even tells Elizabeth, "I am not romantic you know. . . . I ask only a comfortable home."[6] Similarly, Miss Bingley schemes to secure a husband, but unlike Charlotte, she treats other women badly to do so. She repeatedly insults Elizabeth's appearance, manners, and family in an attempt to stain Darcy's opinion of Elizabeth.

These female characters serve as foils to Elizabeth, who refuses to follow society's expectations in seeking a husband.

ARGUMENT THREE

Now the author states how the minor characters differ from Elizabeth: "These female characters serve as foils to Elizabeth, who refuses to follow society's expectations in seeking a husband."

Unlike Mrs. Bennet, Charlotte, or Miss Bingley, Elizabeth does not actively try to secure a marriage. While Mrs. Bennet schemes to marry Jane off to a wealthy man, Elizabeth seeks to avoid the even wealthier Mr. Darcy. Although such a match would give her financial security for life, unlike Charlotte, Elizabeth is not looking only for a comfortable home. She wants a marriage in which she can love and respect her partner. While Miss Bingley throws herself at Darcy with insincere flattery, Elizabeth boldly argues with him, firmly holding to her own opinions and never agreeing with him simply for the sake of pleasing him. But when Elizabeth ultimately realizes she has been wrong about him, she experiences character growth, freely admitting she has been "blind, partial, prejudiced, absurd."[7] She is the only female character to go through such growth in the course of the novel.

Although Elizabeth ultimately marries as women are expected to do, she does so on her own terms. Although women are expected to gratefully accept marriage proposals,

ARGUMENT FOUR

This argument focuses on how Elizabeth acts independently in choosing a husband: "Although Elizabeth ultimately marries as women are expected to do, she does so on her own terms."

Elizabeth turns down not one, but two, offers of marriage, much to the surprise of both men, who never imagined they'd be rejected. In choosing a husband, Elizabeth refuses to give in to the desires of anyone else. She consults only her own feelings. Even when her mother insists she accept Mr. Collins, Elizabeth remains resolute. She even stands up to her social superior, Lady Catherine, when she demands Elizabeth promise not to marry Darcy.

By this time, Elizabeth has had a change of heart regarding Darcy, not because she wants his money or position, but because she has seen his true character and his growth. She first notices it when he treats the Gardiners, her uncle and aunt, as equals at Pemberley. When she learns Darcy is the one who arranged Lydia's marriage, despite the fact it meant paying off his enemy Wickham, she is proud of him. She wonders what could have caused such a drastic change in Darcy's behavior. He tells her she is the one who has sparked his growth by humbling him. It is this change in character—which Elizabeth helped to bring about—that finally enables her to fall in love with Darcy. And not until she is in love with him does she agree to marry him.

Elizabeth's happy ending shows that her position as a strong woman is to be admired and emulated. The other marriages in the novel each have their problems. The calculated marriage of Charlotte and Mr. Collins, although providing a home for Charlotte, gives her little else, and she remains apart from her husband as much as possible. Jane alone among the minor female characters is happily married. As happy as Jane is, though, Elizabeth professes herself to be happier, writing to her Aunt Gardiner that Jane "only smiles, I laugh."[8] Unlike the Bingleys, who are both of a similar temper, Elizabeth's and Darcy's personalities differ, complementing each other. Ultimately, Elizabeth ends up with a husband whom she can love and respect, and it is because of this that her ending is happy. Though the other women, aside from Miss Bingley, have also found husbands, they cannot be as happy as Elizabeth is because they have not acted out of their own strength and independence. Thus, it is ultimately Elizabeth's strength and independence that bring her

ARGUMENT FIVE

The final argument shows how Austen commends Elizabeth's strength: "Elizabeth's happy ending shows that her position as a strong woman is to be admired and emulated."

Elizabeth makes her own, bold decisions and in the end is in love and happier than all other female characters in the novel.

happiness—and it is these qualities that are to be admired and emulated.

During a time when upper-class English women had little choice but to marry, Elizabeth Bennet manages to forge her own way as a strong and independent woman. Unlike the minor female characters in the novel, Elizabeth could be happy with nothing less—and her happy ending implies that other women should strive for the same. It is easy to imagine that had she not met a man whom she could love and respect, Elizabeth would have turned completely against social convention and remained single—much as her creator, Jane Austen, did.

CONCLUSION

The final paragraph concludes the essay by restating the thesis and summing up the arguments, coming back to the idea that Elizabeth's strength is meant to be admired.

THINKING CRITICALLY

Now it's your turn to assess the essay. Consider these questions:

1. The author contends that Elizabeth is a strong female character. Do you agree? Would she be a stronger character if she had remained unmarried?
2. Arguments two and three state that Jane is a foil to Elizabeth. Do you agree? Or are there indications that Elizabeth should act more like her older sister?
3. Which argument do you think is strongest? Which is weakest? Why?

OTHER APPROACHES

The previous essay is just one example of how to analyze the classic novel *Pride and Prejudice*. Another approach might look at the morals of the novel's society. Yet another option is to examine the purpose of irony in the novel.

Manners and Morals in *Pride and Prejudice*

The upper-class characters of *Pride and Prejudice* live by a closely observed set of morals and social rules. A thesis for this approach could be: The formal manners of *Pride and Prejudice* serve more than politeness; the degree to which a character observes those manners is a reflection of his or her moral character.

Irony in *Pride and Prejudice*

Much of the fun of reading *Pride and Prejudice* comes from the ironies that appear throughout the novel. Yet these ironies do more than provide humor. A thesis for this approach could be: The narrative voice, character, dialogue, and situations of *Pride and Prejudice* work together to create an ironic tone that pokes gentle fun at society.

4

AN OVERVIEW OF *THE BOOK THIEF*

Although it was published in 2005, Markus Zusak's *The Book Thief* is already considered a modern classic. Set in Nazi Germany during World War II (1939–1945), the novel is narrated by Death. Death is interested in the story of Liesel Meminger, whom he has seen on several occasions as people around her die. On one of these occasions, he picks up a book she drops. It relates the story of her life, which he shares with the reader.

The Grave Digger's Handbook

Nine-year-old Liesel's story opens on a train, on which she is riding with her mother and brother. While on the train, Liesel's brother dies. Liesel's mother, who is too sick to care for her daughter, leaves Liesel with a foster agency in Munich, Germany. From there, Liesel is taken to stay with her new foster parents, Hans and Rosa

The Book Thief takes place during the time of World War II, when Adolf Hitler strictly ruled Germany.

Liesel and Rudy form a close friendship.

Hubermann, in the nearby town of Molching. Liesel soon begins to call them Mama and Papa. She quickly makes friends with a neighbor boy, Rudy Steiner, who is always asking her for a kiss. She refuses to give him one.

Most nights, Liesel wakes from nightmares of her brother's death. Papa comforts her by reading with her. The first book they read is *The Grave Digger's Handbook*.

A Stolen Book

Like all other ten-year-old German girls, Liesel has to join a group called the Band of German Girls (BDM). There, she practices her "*heil* Hitler," which all Germans are expected to dutifully say in honor of the German führer, or leader, Adolf Hitler. In September 1939, as World War II begins, Hitler's "voice roared from German radios," urging people to victory.[1]

In April 1940, the BDM group is required to attend a bonfire. At the bonfire, the Nazis burn books, magazines, and posters containing pro-Jewish content. A Nazi leader lists the German enemies, including communists. Liesel realizes her family has been persecuted because of her parents' political beliefs. Afterward, Liesel spots an unburned book in the pile of rubble left from the bonfire. She grabs it and hides it under her shirt. Too late, she sees the mayor's wife, Ilsa Hermann, watching her. Ilsa is one of Rosa's laundry customers, and one day when Liesel goes to her house to pick up the laundry, Ilsa invites her in. She leads Liesel to the home's huge library and invites her to read. After that, Liesel spends many summer days reading on the library floor.

Max

Meanwhile, Max Vandenburg, a young Jewish man, makes his way toward Molching. Max has been in hiding because Hitler's army is rounding up Jews and sending them to concentration camps, where many are starved, worked to death, or killed.

Max's father had saved Hans in World War I (1914–1918), and now Hans wants to repay the favor. He sends Max a copy of Hitler's book, *Mein Kampf*, in which he tapes a key to the Hubermann home. When Max arrives, the Hubermanns hide Max in the basement. Max tells stories about his past as a prizefighter and his time in hiding. Liesel and Max grow close and tell each other about their nightmares. When Max is alone in the basement, he imagines he is boxing the führer. Hitler knocks him down, but Max gets back up and launches his own attack. Instead of continuing the fight, the führer uses words to spur his fellow Germans to help him fight this enemy.

For Liesel's twelfth birthday, Max cuts out the pages of *Mein Kampf* and paints them white. Then he writes her a story on the blank pages. The story tells how he and Liesel became friends.

In early June, Ilsa fires Mama, and Liesel feels betrayed. She throws a book at Ilsa's feet and yells at her. Later in the summer, Rudy comes home from a Hitler Youth meeting he is required to attend. His leader there made him do push-ups on a field that had just been fertilized with manure. To make him feel better, Liesel takes him to the Hermanns' house, where she breaks

Earning her nickname, which is also the title of the book, Liesel steals books from the Hermanns' library.

into the library and steals a book called *The Whistler*. Afterward, Rudy calls her a book thief.

Close Calls

As 1942 starts, Max falls ill and unconscious. Every day, Liesel reads to him until she finishes *The Whistler*. Then she returns to the mayor's house and steals a new book, *The Dream Carrier.* Weeks later, Max finally recovers.

Meanwhile, the war moves closer to Molching, with bombs falling in nearby cities. The air-raid sirens continually send the family—except Max—down the street to the shelter in a neighbor's basement. During the raids, Liesel reads aloud to the people gathered in the shelter, keeping them calm.

One day, the Nazis march a parade of Jews through Molching toward Dachau, a concentration camp. Many people gather to watch, including Liesel, Papa, and Rudy. Papa gives a piece of bread to an old Jewish man who can barely walk. A soldier whips both the man and Papa. Afterward, Papa is terrified the Nazis will search his home and find Max. Max leaves, just in case.

The Word Shaker

The Nazi Party comes to recruit Rudy into a new elite training school, but his parents refuse to send him. Soon afterward, Papa is drafted into the German army. Rudy's father is also drafted.

Near Christmastime, Mama gives Liesel a sketchbook that Max left behind for her. Inside, Liesel finds sketches of his life and of stories she's told him.

Liesel resorts to reading to Max as a way to comfort him.

There are even comics mocking the führer. The book's main story is *The Word Shaker*. It is about a man—the führer—who tries to take over the world by planting words across his homeland. He recruits people to tend the words, which grow into forests. But then one day, a young girl takes care of a man who is being mistreated by his homeland. This girl plants her own seed, which grows into a tree that towers over the others. The führer tries to chop it down, but he cannot. The girl stays in the tree many days, and when she finally climbs down, the tree falls, destroying part of the führer's forest.

Leaving Her Story Behind

In April 1943, Papa returns home. That summer, the Nazis march Jews through town. One day, Liesel spots

Max among the Jews. She pushes her way to him and quotes to him from *The Word Shaker*. A soldier whips Max, and then Liesel. Max is forced to walk on, and Rudy pulls Liesel to the side of the road. But she gets up and runs after Max again. Rudy tackles her and won't let her go, even as she punches him.

After this, Liesel stays in bed for three days. When she finally gets up, she tells Rudy about Max and shows him *The Word Shaker*. When Rudy sees a sketch of himself in it, he is surprised that Liesel told Max about him. Liesel realizes she loves Rudy.

At the end of August, Liesel again goes to the mayor's house intending to steal a book. But the sight of the books reminds her of how the führer uses words to spread his hate. She rips up one of the books. Afterward, she feels bad and writes Ilsa a letter to apologize. A few days later, Ilsa gives Liesel a blank book to write in. Liesel begins to spend her nights in the basement, writing her life story.

On October 7, as she is rereading her story in the basement, bombs fall without warning. Liesel is pulled out of the rubble alive, but Mama, Papa, and Rudy are all dead. Liesel kisses Rudy's lips and then sits near Mama's and Papa's bodies until she is led away by the rescue crew. In the confusion, she leaves her story behind, but Death picks it up. He will carry it with him for many years.

Ilsa and the mayor bring Liesel to their home. Later, Rudy's father returns from the war, and Liesel helps him in his tailor shop. After the war, Liesel and Max are reunited. Liesel grows old before Death comes to her. When he arrives, he gives her back the book she wrote—*The Book Thief*.

By October, Liesel completes her book.

5

WORDS AND MORALITY IN *THE BOOK THIEF*

Classic literature often deals with universal themes, such as the nature of good and evil. Moralist criticism looks for the moral values portrayed in a novel and analyzes the work based on what it presents as right or wrong ways of living. Moralist criticism can look at a single character's actions, or it can analyze the morality of an entire society's belief system. In *The Book Thief,* Markus Zusak shows how words have the power to change the world by both establishing and defying the moral code of a society, and he

Markus Zusak's *The Book Thief* is an international best seller.

who march Jews to the concentration camps. As Max sees in his imagined fight with the führer, Hitler calls out to the people for help, and millions of Germans climb into the ring, descending on him with "the fists of an entire nation."[8]

ARGUMENT THREE

In this argument, the author demonstrates how words can also be used for good: "Although words are responsible for the spread of great evil, they are also a potent form of defiance against the moral code of Nazi Germany."

Although words are responsible for the spread of great evil, they are also a potent form of defiance against the moral code of Nazi Germany. Liesel's family does more than shelter Max. They also share their words and stories with him and listen to his. In this land where Germans are supposed to exterminate Jews, words help form a bond between a young German girl and a Jewish man. In the imagined fight with the führer, Max wins because of Liesel's words. Max defies Hitler by painting over the pages of *Mein Kampf* and writing stories about his own life in place of Hitler's words of hate. *The Word Shaker* is the ultimate story of defiance, showing how a young girl manages to fell a small section of the forest of hateful words with her words of love and kindness.

ARGUMENT FOUR

Here, the author elaborates further on the power of words for good. "Words serve not only as a form of defiance; they also have the power to comfort and save."

Words serve not only as a form of defiance; they also have the power to comfort and save. Liesel reads with Papa after her nightmares. She reads to Max when he is sick and to the people gathered in the air-raid shelter when they are scared. In all of these cases, the words bring comfort and a measure of healing. Ironically, the words of Hitler's book, *Mein Kampf*, save Max. The book hides the key to the Hubermann home. Later, when Liesel quotes *The Word Shaker* to Max as he marches, it gives him the hope and courage he needs to continue and survive. In the end, words save Liesel's life. If it weren't for the fact that she was working on her life story when the bombs hit, she would have been killed with everyone else.

Ultimately, *The Book Thief* shows the danger of remaining silent. When the Nazi Party marches through Molching, everyone claps. Some watch the Nazis with fervent pride. But others clap "slow and dutiful" and with "submission."[9] They may not agree with the Nazi Party, but they submit to it to ensure their own survival and peace. Yet, Liesel realizes, "silence was not quiet or calm, and it was not peace."[10]

The novel argues that those who remain silent are just as much to blame for the Holocaust as those who actively attack Jews. During Max's imagined fight with the führer, he is injured not only because people beat him but also because others "let him suffer."[11] They see his pain but do nothing to stop it. In refusing to remain silent, Liesel has a huge impact on those around her. As *The Word Shaker* shows, her tree of words falls on only a small part of the forest, but it succeeds in carving a new path through the trees of hate. In the end, words can hurt. But they can also heal. It is simply a matter of using the right words in the right way.

CONCLUSION

In the final paragraph, the author concludes by restating the thesis. She summarizes the arguments and focuses again on the power of words.

THINKING CRITICALLY

Now it's your turn to assess the essay. Consider these questions:

1. Does the author make a stronger case for words causing evil or fighting against it?
2. Argument One discusses how words are described in the novel. Do you agree that these descriptions help show the power of words? Could they serve any other purpose?
3. People often remain silent in the face of evil to keep themselves and their families safe. Is this morally acceptable? Why or why not?

OTHER APPROACHES

The previous essay is just one example of how to analyze the modern classic *The Book Thief*. Another option might be to examine contradictions in the novel. Still another possibility is to look at gender roles in the novel.

Contradictions in *The Book Thief*

Critics engaged in New Criticism conduct a close reading of a work to determine how literary aspects such as characters, setting, and symbolism work together to create a unified whole. A thesis for this approach could be: Contradictions in the narrator, setting, description, and characters of *The Book Thief* illustrate the contradictory nature of human morality.

Gender Roles in *The Book Thief*

The Book Thief features a wide cast of both male and female characters, many of whom do not act in accordance with stereotypical gender roles. Liesel, for example, is a thief and a bully at times. Between her parents, Hans Hubermann is the affectionate, nurturing figure, while Rosa is gruff and aloof. A thesis for this approach could be: Although set at a time when people were expected to rigidly adhere to prescribed gender roles, *The Book Thief* often turns those gender roles on their heads.

6

AN OVERVIEW OF *THE JOY LUCK CLUB*

Published in 1989, Amy Tan's *The Joy Luck Club* features stories from four mothers and their daughters, who are all in their thirties: Suyuan Woo and her daughter Jing-mei "June" Woo, An-mei Hsu and Rose Hsu Jordan, Lindo and Waverly Jong, and Ying-Ying and Lena St. Clair. Each character narrates two stories, with the exception of Suyuan Woo, who has just died. Her daughter Jing-mei tells Suyuan's stories. The stories take place between roughly the 1930s and the 1980s and relate the mothers' experiences growing

The Joy Luck Club opens with the story of Jing-mei after her mother has passed away.

up in China and immigrating to the United States, as well as the daughters' struggles with their identity as Chinese Americans.

The Joy Luck Club

As the novel opens, Jing-mei's mother, Suyuan Woo, has just died. Jing-mei has been asked to take her place in the Joy Luck Club, a group of four Chinese women who gather to play mah-jongg and talk. Suyuan had formed the original Joy Luck Club in Kweilin, China, when Japan invaded the country in 1937. But Suyuan fled Kweilin when the Japanese threatened to overrun the city. Along the way, she had to abandon everything she carried with her—including her twin babies. When Suyuan immigrated to San Francisco, California, in 1949, she started a new Joy Luck Club. An-mei, Lindo, and Ying-Ying joined.

Now, as Jing-mei plays mah-jongg with the other Joy Luck Club women, they tell her that before Suyuan died, she had been searching for her other daughters—the babies she left behind in Kweilin—and had found an address. The women have written to that address, and now they want Jing-mei to go to China to meet her sisters. Jing-mei wonders what she can tell her sisters

At the Joy Luck Club, Jing-mei learns of her mother's struggles and discovers she has twin siblings.

about her mother. The other women are distressed at the thought of a daughter not knowing her mother. They fear that the same is true of their own daughters.

An-mei and Rose

An-mei's story begins in China, where she is raised by her aunt, uncle, and grandmother, whom she calls Popo. Her father is dead, and a wealthy merchant named Wu Tsing has forced her mother to become his concubine. Because of this, Popo has disowned An-mei's mother and will not even allow An-mei to speak her name. But after Popo dies, An-mei goes to live with her mother, who eventually takes her own life. An-mei grows up, moves to the United States, and marries George Hsu. They have seven children, including Rose.

In the present, Rose is trying to figure out how to tell her mother that she and her husband, Ted, are getting divorced. She doesn't expect to find a way to save her marriage. But her mother tells her she must try. When she receives the divorce papers from Ted, Rose can't decide whether to sign them. So she crawls into bed for three days. On the fourth day, her mother calls and tells her to speak up for herself. Rose takes her advice and tells Ted she's keeping the house.

Lindo and Waverly

Lindo's story starts when she is two years old, and the village matchmaker arranges her engagement to Tyan-yu. At the age of 12, she is sent to live with her future husband's family. For the next four years, Tyan-yu's family treats Lindo as a servant. When she is 16, she and Tyan-yu are married. Although she is afraid to sleep with Tyan-yu, he never touches her, and she comes to love him like a brother. Lindo's mother-in-law grows angry that Lindo has not produced an heir, so Lindo tricks her mother-in-law into sending her away by saying the ancestors told her in a dream that Tyan-yu will die if he remains married to her.

After working for 12 years as a telephone operator, Lindo moves to the United States. In San Francisco, she works in a fortune cookie factory. Her friend An-mei introduces her to Tin Jong. Lindo wants Tin to propose, so she gives him a fortune cookie about making a home with a spouse. Lindo and Tin marry and have three children, including Waverly.

Growing up in San Francisco's Chinatown, Waverly teaches herself to play chess. She eventually gets good enough to enter national tournaments. Lindo is proud of her daughter and introduces her wherever they go. To Waverly, it seems as if her mother is trying to claim

Lindo proudly shows off Waverly's chess accomplishments to everyone they meet.

credit for her success, and one day, she yells at her mother for showing her off. After that, Lindo no longer cheers for Waverly or boasts about her. By the time she is 14, Waverly quits playing chess.

Now Waverly is divorced from a Chinese-American man and trying to work up the nerve to tell her mother that she's getting remarried to a Caucasian man named Rich. She thinks her overly critical mother hates Rich because she is always saying horrible things about him. One day Waverly goes to her mother's house to confront her, but she finds her mother sleeping and suddenly worries that she's dead. When Lindo wakes up, Waverly tells her that she's marrying Rich. Lindo says she already knew, without needing to be told.

Before the wedding, Lindo and Waverly get their hair done together. They talk about Waverly and Rich's planned honeymoon to China. Waverly is afraid she'll "blend in so well they think I'm one of them."[1] But Lindo tells her they will know she's an outsider, just by the way she carries herself.

Ying-Ying and Lena

Ying-Ying is born to a wealthy family in Wushi, China. When she is 16, she falls in love and gets married. Her

Ying-Ying is afterward scarred by her relationship with her first husband.

marriage changes her from a wild and independent girl into "a stranger to myself."[2] Everything she does, she does for her husband. But then he leaves her to live with another woman. She hates him so much she aborts the child they conceived.

She moves to the country to live with relatives before later moving to Shanghai to work as a shop girl. While working there, she meets an American man named Clifford St. Clair. He courts her for four years. She pretends to be pleased with the cheap trinkets he gives her, and when he proposes, Ying-Ying says yes, even though she doesn't love him. The two don't even speak the same language. They move to the United

States, where Ying-Ying raises a daughter, Lena, while struggling with depression.

At school, few people even realize Lena is Chinese because of her English-Irish heritage from her father. When Lena is ten, her mother becomes pregnant, but the child is stillborn. Afterward, Ying-Ying falls apart. Lena spends most of her time feeling scared and alone.

In the present, Lena is married to Harold, and the two work for the same architectural firm. Harold is a partner, while Lena is an associate, even though Lena came up with the premise for the business. Now, Ying-Ying is visiting. Ying-Ying examines a list on the refrigerator that keeps track of exactly how much each of them spends. The two split the cost of most things equally, even though Lena makes less money. Ying-Ying asks why Lena has to share the cost of ice cream with her husband when she doesn't even eat it.

Later, after Ying-Ying is in bed, Lena tells Harold she won't help pay for ice cream anymore. When Harold agrees, Lena shouts at him for being so fair and says she's tired of working so hard to make things come out even. Lena hears a crash from Ying-Ying's room and goes up to find that a vase has broken. Ying-Ying's story makes it clear that she broke the vase on purpose to get her daughter's attention. She fears that Lena has no chi, or spirit, and has decided to tell her about her own life in the hope that it will help her daughter find her chi.

Jing-mei

When Jing-mei is a child, her mother tries to convince her that in the United States people can be anything. When Waverly becomes a chess star, Suyuan decides that her daughter should also be a prodigy. She tests Jing-mei's abilities in different areas. But Jing-mei never meets her mother's expectations. Eventually, Suyuan enrolls Jing-mei in piano lessons, but the piano teacher is deaf, so Jing-mei doesn't practice. Still, Suyuan brags to Lindo about Jing-mei's skills. Lindo brings her family to hear Jing-mei play in a talent show, but the performance is a disaster. Afterward, Jing-mei refuses to play. When her mother tries to make her, Jing-mei says she wishes she were dead, like her mother's other daughters. After that, her mother never mentions the piano again, until Jing-mei's thirtieth birthday, when she offers the instrument to her. After her mother's death, Jing-mei travels to China to meet her sisters. As she hugs them, she realizes the Chinese part of her has been there all along—it's her family.

7

STEREOTYPES AND IDENTITY IN *THE JOY LUCK CLUB*

The experience of being an outsider, as well as the search for identity, is a common characteristic of classic literature. This is especially true in novels dealing with the experiences of minority groups, such as immigrants. Critical race theory examines cultural perceptions of race. It looks at racial stereotypes and how ideas about race shape an individual's identity.

When it was published in 1989, *The Joy Luck Club* was praised for its presentation of the Chinese-American experience.

In *The Joy Luck Club*, author Amy Tan brings to light Chinese and American racial stereotypes.

Later critics, however, argued the novel perpetuates stereotypes about the Chinese culture and people. But the stereotypes in the novel serve a purpose in enhancing the theme of cultural identity. Although Amy Tan uses racial stereotypes in *The Joy Luck Club,* she does so in a way that allows her to explore the Chinese and American cultures and show that only by accepting both cultures can the characters forge their true identities.

In many ways, the mothers in *The Joy Luck Club* exemplify traditional stereotypes of Chinese women, while they see their daughters as stereotypical Americans. The mothers all speak broken English and recite superstitions. Many of them fall into the category of the stereotypical Chinese female, as women who are

THESIS

The thesis comes at the end of the introduction: "Although Amy Tan uses racial stereotypes in *The Joy Luck Club,* she does so in a way that allows her to explore the Chinese and American cultures and show that only by accepting both cultures can the characters forge their true identities." The thesis introduces the arguments the author will make.

ARGUMENT ONE

The first argument outlines the stereotypes the novel perpetuates: "In many ways, the mothers in *The Joy Luck Club* exemplify traditional stereotypes of Chinese women, while they see their daughters as stereotypical Americans."

weak, subservient, and in need of rescuing by a man. As a child, An-mei is "taught to desire nothing, to swallow other people's misery, to eat [her] own bitterness."[1] For Lindo, subservience begins when she is only two years old and is pledged to be married to Tyan-yu. When she goes to live with her future husband's family, she is forced to work as a servant. Later, when she and Tyan-yu are married, Lindo meekly takes the blame for not producing an heir, despite the fact that her husband has no sexual interest in her. Meanwhile, in marrying Clifford St. Clair, Ying-Ying gives up her chi, or spirit. She also loses her voice, since she and her husband don't speak the same language. As a result, her husband puts words in her mouth.

Despite their quiet subservience, some of the mothers also fit the stereotype of Chinese women as manipulative and seductive dragon ladies. Ying-Ying knows she doesn't love Clifford St. Clair, yet she uses her feminine charms to snag him. When he gives her cheap gifts that are nothing compared with the riches among which she grew up, she accepts them with just the right amount of protest to please him. When she is ready for him to propose, she speaks in a trembling voice and lets herself become pale and thin, "a wounded animal" for him to save.[2] Lindo, too, uses manipulation to secure a proposal, presenting her boyfriend with a fortune cookie about marriage to make him "realize his intentions."[3]

In addition, the mothers fit the stereotype of Chinese women as strict mothers who try to control their daughters' lives. Determined to make Jing-mei a prodigy, Suyuan forces her to take ridiculous tests to discover her hidden talent. When she can't find one, she decides her daughter will be a piano prodigy. Lindo, too, acts as the overbearing mother when it comes to Waverly's chess playing. Even when their daughters are grown, all of the mothers try to tell them how to run their lives to some extent.

One of the reasons the mothers feel the need to control their daughters' lives is that they see their children as stereotypical Americans who grow up "speaking only English and swallowing more Coca-Cola than sorrow."[4] They collectively worry their daughters have no Chinese character. As Lindo says of her daughter Waverly, "Only her skin and her hair are Chinese. Inside—she is all American-made."[5] In addition, the mothers see their daughters as lazy Americans who are not willing to work to live up to expectations.

These stereotypical behaviors cause the daughters to reject their mothers, along with their Chinese heritage. The daughters resent their mothers' interference in their lives. The girls make fun of their mothers for mispronouncing English words. Waverly says she's embarrassed by her mother and tells people Lindo came to the United States "on a slow boat from China."[6] Their rejection of their mothers also leads the daughters to reject their Chinese heritage. Lena pushes on her eyes to try to make them rounder. Jing-mei goes by the name *June* and tries to deny she is Chinese. Part of the reason the daughters reject both their heritage and their mothers is because they don't understand either. Although the daughters speak some Chinese and the mothers know some English, they often misunderstand each other's intentions. Because of these misunderstandings, the daughters dismiss the wisdom their mothers try to hand down to them as "just more of [their] Chinese superstitions."[7]

ARGUMENT TWO

The second argument highlights the effect of these stereotypes on the characters in the novel: "These stereotypical behaviors cause the daughters to reject their mothers, along with their Chinese heritage."

ARGUMENT THREE

The third argument shows how the stereotypes are later overturned: "As the characters grow during the course of the novel, they break out of these stereotypes to some extent, and in doing so begin to find their true identities."

As the characters grow during the course of the novel, they break out of these stereotypes to some extent, and in doing so begin to find their true identities. Ying-Ying finds her voice and tells her daughter her story. In doing so, she feels her chi returning and hopes she will pass it on to her daughter. Lindo and Suyuan break free of their roles as overbearing parents as well. The daughters, too, let go of some of their stereotypical American behaviors. Jing-mei starts playing the piano again and realizes she probably could have done more to live up to her mother's expectations. The daughters also begin to show more respect for their mothers. They listen to their mothers' stories, even if they don't always understand them.

ARGUMENT FOUR

The final argument shows how the daughters discover their true identity: "It is not until the daughters embrace the Chinese part of themselves that they can deal with their problems and forge identities as authentic Chinese Americans."

It is not until the daughters embrace the Chinese part of themselves that they can deal with their problems and forge identities as authentic Chinese Americans. As they listen to their mothers' stories, the daughters begin to respect them. This in turn allows them to appreciate the wisdom of the heritage their mothers are trying to transmit to them. The lessons they learn from their mothers enable the daughters to begin solving their own problems. An-mei's stories encourage Rose to tell her husband she's going to keep the house in the divorce. Ying-Ying's talk with her daughter about her first marriage leads Lena to confront the problems in her own marriage. The ultimate sign of the daughters' acceptance of their Chinese heritage is Jing-mei's trip to meet her

By the end of novel, each daughter has come to better understand her mother and form a closer bond.

half-sisters. As soon as she enters China, she feels herself becoming Chinese, and although this would have upset her at one point in her life, it now pleases her. Finally, when she meets her sisters, she realizes the part of her that is Chinese is her family.

When the girls accept their Chinese blood, they forge identities as authentic Chinese Americans. By the end of the novel, each daughter has come to embrace the fact that a large part of her identity is wrapped up in her heritage. With that new sense of identity intact and with the support of their Chinese mothers, the daughters can face their problems.

CONCLUSION

The conclusion restates the thesis and summarizes the arguments to show how *The Joy Luck Club* uses and overcomes stereotypes to bring its characters to an understanding of their true identity.

THINKING CRITICALLY

Now it's your turn to assess the essay. Consider these questions:

1. Does the author present a strong thesis with persuasive arguments? Would you change any of the arguments to make a stronger case?
2. Do you agree with the author's conclusion that the daughters ultimately come to accept and respect their mothers as well as their heritage? Are there any hints that they might still resist being Chinese?
3. Can identity exist apart from race, or is it necessary for a person to accept his or her heritage in order to forge an identity?

OTHER APPROACHES

The previous essay is just one example of how to analyze *The Joy Luck Club*. Another approach might look at how the novel was influenced by Amy Tan's life. Yet another idea is to consider the portrayal of women in the novel.

Weaving Fact and Fiction in *The Joy Luck Club*

Many events in *The Joy Luck Club* are based on Amy Tan's own life and family. Similar to Jing-mei, Amy Tan has half-sisters in China, and similar to all of the daughters in the novel, Tan struggled through a difficult relationship with her Chinese mother. A thesis for this approach could be: By incorporating experiences from her own life into *The Joy Luck Club*, Amy Tan both personalizes and universalizes cultural, generational, and individual conflicts and highlights the importance of family and heritage in resolving these conflicts.

Women in *The Joy Luck Club*

In many Asian cultures, families are matriarchal, or headed by women. The focus on the mother-daughter relationships in *The Joy Luck Club* illustrates the power of female bonds. A thesis for this approach could be: Although the daughters of *The Joy Luck Club* initially reject their mothers, it is only by bonding with them that they are empowered to become strong women.

8

OVERVIEWS OF *BRAVE NEW WORLD* AND *THE HANDMAID'S TALE*

When it was first published in 1932, Aldous Huxley's dystopian novel *Brave New World* was widely criticized as weak, shallow, and irrelevant. Since that time, however, the novel has risen to the status of a classic, as readers have identified with its pessimistic view of human nature, consumerism, and the desire for stability.

Life in the World State

Brave New World is set in London in year A.F. 632. A.F. stands for "After Ford," since time in the novel is marked from the date Henry Ford introduced the Model T automobile. The society is ruled by an all-controlling

Aldous Huxley was a novelist and philosopher.

government known as the World State, which took over after a massive war devastated the globe.

Everything in the World State is directed toward maintaining stability. Babies are grown in bottles in factories. Conditions in the bottles are carefully controlled so babies will develop into members of different castes, or groups based on social rank: Alphas, Betas, Gammas, Deltas, and Epsilons. Alphas are given optimal conditions to develop into athletic and intelligent individuals. Babies destined to belong to the lower castes are grown in batches of up to 100 clones. While still in the bottle, they are exposed to harmful substances to stunt their growth and intelligence. After being decanted, or hatched, from their bottles, the babies and young children are conditioned with hypnopedia, or sleep teaching. Each student is conditioned to believe his or her class is the best but that the others are also necessary. Anyone can tell at a glance what class another person belongs to, just by the color of his or her clothing. Members of separate classes rarely interact.

Promiscuity is encouraged and enforced in the World State, and even children are taught to take part in erotic games. The goal is to prevent people from

The government administers Soma to members of the World State as a means of controlling society.

forming emotional attachments that can cause strong feelings. Soma, a drug that sends users on a "holiday from reality," is offered to everyone as another way of preventing people from experiencing strong emotions.[1]

Lenina and Bernard

Lenina Crowne works at the hatchery where babies are grown. She makes a date with Bernard Marx, an Alpha-Plus psychologist who also works at the hatchery. Unlike other Alphas, Bernard is short and unattractive, possibly because of a mistake in the factory when he was in the bottle. Because he is different from other Alphas, Bernard feels isolated. His one friend is Helmholtz

Watson, who also feels different. Watson's isolation is due not to a physical shortcoming but rather to a "mental excess."[2]

Lenina finds Bernard odd for not taking Soma and not wanting to sleep with her on their first date. But she convinces him to do both. Afterward, Bernard wishes they had waited. He craves a real relationship with Lenina and wants to act as an adult rather than an infant who must have his desires fulfilled immediately.

The Savage Reservation

Bernard asks his boss, the director of the hatchery, for permission to go to the Savage Reservation, an area in New Mexico that has not been civilized by the World State, with Lenina. The director reveals that he took a girl to the reservation once. But the girl got lost, and he returned to London without her. After revealing this, the director reprimands Bernard for not acting more like an infant in his relationships and warns that if his behavior doesn't improve, he will be transferred to Iceland.

Bernard and Lenina go to the Savage Reservation. After watching a ceremony in which a young man is repeatedly whipped, Lenina and Bernard meet John, a young man who says he's never been accepted on the reservation because his mother, Linda, came from the Other Place, meaning the World State. Bernard immediately realizes John must be the director's son, and he arranges to bring him and his mother to London.

Blackmail

When Bernard returns to London, the director says he's being sent to Iceland. In response, Bernard brings in Linda and John. The director immediately resigns. Bringing back John makes Bernard wildly popular, and people clamor to attend his parties, where John—or the Savage, as most people call him—is the main attraction. Bernard now has a different woman every night. He continues to criticize the government, mostly because doing so makes him feel important.

Meanwhile, John has a hard time adjusting to civilization. The sight of hundreds of identical lower-caste workers sickens him. He refuses to take Soma and resists the temptation to sleep with Lenina, since he believes in chastity before marriage. One night, John refuses to attend Bernard's party. The disappointed guests immediately leave, and Bernard finds himself once again isolated.

Unhappy Ending

John tells Lenina he loves her. He wants to marry her, as people do on the reservation, but she just wants to sleep with him. When she pulls off her clothes, he threatens to kill her if she doesn't get out of his sight. Immediately afterward, John receives a phone call informing him that Linda—who has been on a permanent Soma holiday since she arrived from the reservation—is sick. While he's visiting her, she dies.

Afterward, John sees a group of Deltas being given their Soma rations. He grabs the Soma and throws it out the window, sparking a riot. Bernard and Helmholtz arrive to rescue John. Helmholtz jumps into the fray and helps John throw more Soma out the window, while Bernard hangs back, unsure what to do. The police take John, Helmholtz, and Bernard to see Mustapha Mond, one of the World Controllers.

The Controller sends Bernard and Helmholtz to an island, which he says is more of a reward than a punishment, since they will meet other unorthodox people there. He refuses to send John, however, because he wants to continue the social experiment of having a Savage in civilization.

John moves to a lighthouse far from civilization. A photographer discovers his location and secretly makes a film of John whipping himself in an attempt to purify his mind against lustful thoughts of Lenina. The film is turned into a feely—a movie that involves all five senses—and soon people flock to see the Savage at his home. They chant for him to get out his whip. When Lenina arrives, he does so, whipping himself and her. The crowd soon joins in, whipping each other in what becomes a sensual act. When John wakes up the next morning, he is stricken. That night, when the crowds descend on the lighthouse, they find that he has hung himself.

The Handmaid's Tale

Margaret Atwood's 1985 novel, *The Handmaid's Tale*, is also a dystopian work. It depicts a future world in which the Republic of Gilead has taken the place of the former United States. It came to power following the assassination of the president and Congress, apparently by Islamic militants. Women in Gilead are forbidden from working, having money, or even reading. Because environmental catastrophe and war have led to infertility and a sharp decline in the human population, the remaining fertile women are forced to serve as handmaids. A handmaid's job is to sleep with powerful men who have infertile wives. Any children the handmaids give birth to become the property of the men and their wives.

Life as a Handmaid

The novel opens with the narrator—whose real name readers never learn—at a women's center. The women there are all handmaids, and they are patrolled by women known as Aunts. The Aunts carry cattle prods to punish any women who disobey the rules. From the Women's Center, the narrator is sent to live with a man named Fred, whom she calls the Commander. Her name becomes Offred, since she belongs to Fred ("of Fred"). The Commander's wife is Serena Joy, and the family also employs two Marthas, or servants, and a chauffeur named Nick.

Offred spends her days in her room, except when she goes out to do the shopping. Her uniform is a full-bodied red dress and a white head covering blocks her face from view. While shopping, a handmaid from another house, Ofglen, accompanies Offred. The two are paired to spy on each other so neither can break the rules.

All handmaids are forced to wear red dresses.

The Ceremony

When Offred goes to her required monthly checkup, the doctor offers to sleep with her to help her get pregnant. Offred declines, saying it's too dangerous. If she were caught, she would be killed. But she also knows that if she doesn't get pregnant soon, she will be sent to the Colonies, a wretched place for those who refuse to conform to society's rules.

After returning from the doctor, Offred naps. She dreams about her husband, Luke, and their daughter. She remembers their failed escape attempt, in which Luke was shot and her daughter taken. When she wakes, Offred has to participate in the Ceremony. The entire household gathers to listen to the Commander read the Bible. Afterward, the Commander has intercourse with Offred. The wife must be present.

Getting around the System

The night after the Ceremony, the Commander asks Offred to meet him in his office, even though it is illegal for her to be alone with him. When Offred arrives, he asks her to play Scrabble. This, too, is illegal, since women are not allowed to read or write, but Offred plays. Before she returns to her room, the Commander requests a kiss. After this, Offred goes to the Commander's office a few nights a week.

One day in July, Serena Joy tells Offred that perhaps she should try getting pregnant by the chauffeur, Nick. As a reward for her agreement, Offred is given a cigarette and a match. She hides the match under her mattress, thinking about burning the house down.

Not long afterward, the Commander sneaks Offred into a brothel called Jezebel's. There, Offred sees an old friend named Moira, who had escaped from the Women's Center by stabbing one of the Aunts and stealing her clothes. Moira tells Offred that she remained free for eight or nine months after her escape, but the authorities then caught her. They made her watch a video that showed women in the Colonies cleaning up toxic waste and radioactive materials. The authorities gave Moira the choice of going to the Colonies or working as a prostitute, and she chose prostitution.

After talking with Moira, *left*, Offred, *right*, learns more about the treatment of women in Gilead.

When Offred returns from talking with Moira, the Commander rents a room in the brothel and sleeps with Offred. When she gets home, Offred meets with the Commander's wife, who leads her to Nick so she can sleep with him. Afterward, Offred goes to Nick's room night after night without the Commander's wife knowing. She tells Nick about her life before and even gives him her real name. For his part, Nick talks little.

Meanwhile, Ofglen reveals to Offred that she is part of a resistance movement. She tries to convince Offred to search the Commander's office for information that can help the resistance, but Offred says it's too risky. When Ofglen says they could get her out, Offred realizes she doesn't want to leave Nick.

Beginning or End?

One day, all the women are required to attend a meeting called a Women's Salvaging. Two handmaids and a wife are hanged. Afterward, the handmaids are instructed to beat a man who has been accused of raping a pregnant woman. Ofglen rushes forward to kick him in the head. Ofglen tells Offred that the man was part of the resistance, and she killed him quickly as an act of mercy.

Later that day, Offred learns Ofglen has been replaced. The new handmaid says Ofglen hanged herself when she saw the black van coming to arrest her. The news makes Offred realize she will do anything to stay alive.

When Offred gets home, Serena Joy confronts her. She knows Offred has been sleeping with the Commander behind her back. As Offred hears the black van coming to arrest her, Nick comes into her room. He tells her that the men in the van are from the resistance. Offred goes with them, even though she's not sure if she can trust Nick. She wonders if this will be the end or a new beginning.

The final chapter features a speech given by a professor in the year 2195, approximately 200 years after the events of the story. Gilead has since fallen and been replaced by a society that doesn't face the same population pressures. But researchers continue to study Gileadean history. The professor says he thinks the story of the Handmaid's Tale—which was recorded on audio tapes—is legitimate. Although he has been unable to identify Offred, he believes she probably escaped at least long enough to record her story, even if she may have been recaptured later.

9

POWER AND CONTROL

Struggles of class, wealth, and power are common themes in classic literature. Marxist criticism considers how social class is presented in a work of literature. Marxist critics examine who holds the power in the work and how he or she maintains that power. Critics study how social classes interact and whether anyone rebels against the social structure.

At face value, *Brave New World* and *The Handmaid's Tale* present two very different futures. In one, everyone lives in bliss, while in the other, people live in fear. But the totalitarian governments of the World State in *Brave New World* and Gilead in *The Handmaid's Tale* have more in common than it may at first appear. Although the World State and Gilead maintain power in different ways, both demonstrate how totalitarian regimes use indoctrination

Though published more than 50 years after *Brave New World,* Margaret Atwood's *The Handmaid's Tale* portrays a society's control in many similar ways.

THESIS STATEMENT

The thesis statement of this essay focuses on how totalitarian governments maintain power: "Although the World State and Gilead maintain power in different ways, both demonstrate how totalitarian regimes use indoctrination and strict class divisions to strip individuals of their identities and their will to rebel."

ARGUMENT ONE

The first argument presents an overview of the governments in the two novels: "Both the World State and Gilead came into existence as a result of war and seek to maintain social stability."

and strict class divisions to strip individuals of their identities and their will to rebel.

Both the World State and Gilead came into existence as a result of war and seek to maintain social stability. The World State was created after war and economic collapse devastated the planet. Afterward, "people were ready to have even their appetites controlled. . . . Anything for a quiet life."[1] Now, the World State's primary purpose is to maintain stability. In order to achieve that stability, the World State seeks to keep people content by means of genetic engineering, hypnopedia, and Soma. Gilead, too, rose to power out of instability. This society was formed in place of the former United States after the president and Congress were killed. Afterward, the Constitution was suspended, but as in the World State, few people protested. They were just grateful that someone was providing direction. Unlike the World State, the government of Gilead doesn't care about happiness. Its harsh laws focus on morality as a means of bringing about stability and restoring the depleted population.

Despite their differences, both societies rely on strict class divisions. In the World State, class divisions are established in the hatchery, as babies of different castes are subjected to different conditions. Even clothing signals class differences. In Gilead, class divisions are based not on heredity but on gender and position. The most powerful members of society are men such as the Commander, who have a part in maintaining the world order. Among the women, the most powerful are the wives, although their power is limited by the fact that they cannot have children and therefore cannot fulfill the main goal of their society. The handmaids, on the other hand, can have children but are powerless, forced to sleep with whichever man they are assigned to. Other women, such as the

ARGUMENT TWO

The second argument looks at social classes in the novels: "Despite their differences, both societies rely on strict class divisions."

Marthas, have even less power. As in *Brave New World*, the color of clothing denotes class. The handmaids wear red, for example, while the Marthas wear green. This makes it easy to tell on first meeting a woman where she fits within the power structure.

ARGUMENT THREE

The author next looks at the effects of class divisions on individuals: "In both worlds, these class divisions strip individuals of their identities and prevent them from forming meaningful relationships."

In both worlds, these class divisions strip individuals of their identities and prevent them from forming meaningful relationships. The whole premise of the World State is preserving the good of the community by keeping people from acting as individuals. Any deviation from conditioned behavior is considered unorthodox. As the director says, unorthodoxy is more dangerous than murder, since "murder kills only the individual" while "unorthodoxy . . . strikes at Society itself."[2] In addition, promiscuity prevents strong attachments that can lead to emotions and instability.

For the handmaids in Gilead, individuality is stripped when they are given names based on those of their masters. Class differences also prevent people from forming meaningful relationships. Although they work in the same home, Marthas are not allowed to socialize with handmaids, for example. Even with Ofglen, another handmaid, Offred has to be cautious. The two talk about the resistance, but they never grow close enough to tell each other their real names. Offred's closest relationship is with Nick, but even that remains superficial. Although she tells him about her life before—and even her real name—he "seems indifferent to most of what I have to say, alive only to the possibilities of my body."[3]

Indoctrination and fear further ensure loyalty to the state. In *Brave New World*, indoctrination occurs from birth, as babies are subjected to hypnopedia. But the indoctrination doesn't stop when they are adults. Forms of entertainment such as the news, music, and the feelies are produced by the government propaganda department. Fear is less prevalent in the World State, but it hovers in the background. Violence is never a concern, since the World State long ago realized force does not maintain

ARGUMENT FOUR

The fourth argument focuses on other government methods of maintaining control: "Indoctrination and fear further ensure loyalty to the state."

stability. Instead, anyone who doesn't conform to society faces the threat of being sent away.

In Gilead, on the other hand, fear is the driving force behind indoctrination. Religion is cited as the foundation for the new world order, and the Commander reads from the Bible before the Ceremony, citing only passages that seem to support the idea of using handmaids. As in the World State, news reports in Gilead serve to further indoctrinate. Despite the indoctrination, it is impossible to tell who is a true believer in Gilead and who conforms to society's rules out of fear of banishment to the Colonies or public hanging.

ARGUMENT FIVE

The final argument shows how the governments' measures keep people from rebelling: "Ultimately, both governments' methods of control lead to apathy on the part of citizens, preventing wide-scale rebellion and allowing the leaders to maintain power."

Ultimately, both governments' methods of control lead to apathy on the part of citizens, preventing wide-scale rebellion and allowing the leaders to maintain power. In *Brave New World*, the majority of people are happy with their situation and have no desire to turn against the government. Even the major characters who question the world order never take action against the government. Bernard at first seems like a rebel. He seeks a real relationship with Lenina and wants to feel something—anything—strongly and refuses to take Soma. Yet his dissatisfaction with the system fades as soon as he becomes popular. Later, when he is again isolated, he turns to Soma to deal with the strong feelings of unhappiness he had earlier professed to desire. And when he is banished for speaking out against the government, he begs to remain in the society he had so ardently criticized. It is John, the outsider, who takes the most drastic action against the World State, throwing Soma rations out the window. But rather than leading a rebellion, he withdraws to an isolated lighthouse. When civilization finds him, he kills himself.

In Gilead, too, most people accept the world order without question. Rebelling is too dangerous. A few characters resist for a time but ultimately give in. Of all the characters, Ofglen is the most active in the resistance. But when her involvement in the movement is discovered, she kills herself. Moira, too, begins as an active rebel. She fights back against the Aunts and even manages to escape the Women's Center. But by the time Offred sees her at Jezebel's, Moira has become indifferent, as if she has accepted her situation. When

Offred first arrives at the Commander's house, she makes it clear that she intends to survive this ordeal and escape. But her desire to resist is slowly worn away. When she starts sleeping with Nick, she no longer even desires to escape. After Ofglen's death, Offred is so relieved to be alive that she vows to do anything, as long as she can "keep on living, in any form," even if that means letting others use her body as they wish.[4] As she waits for what she thinks will be her arrest, Offred takes no action, even though she has a match under her mattress with which she could burn down the house.

Despite their different methods of governing, the World State and Gilead have found a foolproof way to maintain control with powerful weapons such as class divisions, fear, and indoctrination. Both will continue to rule until someone comes along who is strong enough to stand up against them.

CONCLUSION

The final paragraph concludes the essay by restating the thesis and summarizing the arguments. It reflects the idea that although these totalitarian governments are different, both will continue to maintain their power.

THINKING CRITICALLY

Now it's your turn to assess the essay. Consider these questions:

1. The author argues that social classes contribute to the governments' ability to maintain control. Do you agree? What would happen if these social classes were abolished?
2. Which argument is the most persuasive? Are there any that need more development?
3. Does Gilead or the World State more successfully rule its people? Why?

OTHER APPROACHES

The previous essay is just one example of how to analyze *Brave New World* and *The Handmaid's Tale*. Another approach might look at the novels from a feminist perspective. Still another option is to consider the moral values in these novels.

Feminism in *Brave New World* and *The Handmaid's Tale*

The Handmaid's Tale is often read as a feminist work, while *Brave New World* has been criticized as anti-feminist. Yet both novels present women as sexual objects. A thesis for this approach could be: While Atwood's presentation of women as sexual objects is a conscious protest against the objectification of women in the 1980s, Huxley's portrayal of women is a reflection of the misogynistic views of the 1930s.

Morality in *Brave New World* and *The Handmaid's Tale*

Dystopian novels generally present a pessimistic view of human nature and its failure to uphold moral values. A thesis for this approach might be: Both Atwood and Huxley see humanity moving toward an ever more corrupt moral system, but the two authors' ideas of corrupt and immoral vary drastically.

ANALYZE IT!

Now that you have learned different approaches to analyzing a work, are you ready to perform your own analysis? You have read that this type of evaluation can help you look at literature in a new way and make you pay attention to certain issues you may not have otherwise recognized. So, why not use one of these approaches to consider a fresh take on your favorite work?

First, choose a philosophy, critical theory, or other approach and consider which work or works you want to analyze. Remember the approach you choose is a springboard for asking questions about the works.

Next, write a specific question that relates to your approach or philosophy. Then you can form your thesis, which should provide the answer to that question. Your thesis is the most important part of your analysis and offers an argument about the work, considering its characters, plot, or literary techniques, or what it says about society or the world. Recall that the thesis statement typically appears at the very end of the introductory paragraph of your essay. It is usually only one sentence long.

After you have written your thesis, find evidence to back it up. Good places to start are in the work itself or in journals or articles that discuss what other people have said about it. You may also want to read about the author or creator's life so you can get a sense of what factors may have affected the creative process. This can be especially useful if you are considering how the work connects to history or the author's intent.

You should also explore parts of the book that seem to disprove your thesis and create an argument against them. As you do this, you might want to address what others have written about the book. Their quotes may help support your claim.

Before you start analyzing a work, think about the different arguments made in this book. Reflect on how evidence supporting the thesis was presented. Did you find that some of the techniques used to back up the arguments were more convincing than others? Try these methods as you prove your thesis in your own analysis paper.

When you are finished writing your analysis, read it over carefully. Is your thesis statement understandable? Do the supporting arguments flow logically, with the topic of each paragraph clearly stated? Can you add any information that would present your readers with a stronger argument in favor of your thesis? Were you able to use quotes from the book, as well as from other critics, to enhance your ideas?

Did you see the work in a new light?

GLOSSARY

COMMUNIST

A person who believes in communism, an economic system based on the elimination of private ownership of factories, land, and other means of economic production.

CONCUBINE

An unmarried woman who has sexual intercourse and lives with a man and his wife or wives.

CONSUMERISM

A theory that promotes an increase in the purchase and use of goods and services.

DYSTOPIAN

A type of utterly horrible or degraded society that is generally headed to an irreversible oblivion.

FOIL

A literary character whose basic qualities contrast with those of the protagonist.

INDOCTRINATION

The act of teaching someone to fully accept the ideas, opinions, and beliefs of a particular group and not to consider other ideas, opinions, or beliefs.

PROMISCUITY

Having or involving too many sexual partners.

PROPAGANDA

Information that carries facts or details slanted to favor a single point of view or political bias.

REGIME

A governing power.

STEREOTYPE

An often unfair and untrue belief that many people have about all people or things with a particular characteristic—for example, gender or race.

STEWARD

A person who manages the land and property of another person.

SYMBOLISM

The use of words, objects, or ideas to stand for something else; symbols often stand for something abstract, such as peace or innocence.

THEME

The subject or main idea of a creative work.

TOTALITARIAN

A type of government that is centralized and dictatorial.

ADDITIONAL
RESOURCES

SELECTED BIBLIOGRAPHY

Atwood, Margaret. *The Handmaid's Tale*. New York: Anchor, 1986. Print.

Austen, Jane. *Pride and Prejudice*. New York: Penguin, 1985. Print.

Huxley, Aldous. *Brave New World*. New York: HarperPerennial, 1998. Print.

Lynn, Steven. *Texts and Contexts: Writing about Literature with Critical Theory*. New York: Longman, 1998. Print.

Moler, Kenneth. *Pride and Prejudice: A Study in Artistic Economy*. Boston: Twayne, 1989. Print.

Tan, Amy. *The Joy Luck Club*. New York: Penguin, 1989. Print.

Wiener, Gary. *Women's Issues in Amy Tan's* The Joy Luck Club. Detroit: Greenhaven, 2008. Print.

Zusak, Markus. *The Book Thief*. New York: Knopf, 2005. Print.

FURTHER READINGS

Mussari, Mark. *Amy Tan*. New York: Marshall Cavendish Benchmark, 2011. Print.

Reef, Catherine. *Jane Austen: A Life Revealed*. Boston: Clarion Books/Houghton Mifflin Harcourt, 2011. Print.

WEBSITES

To learn more about Essential Literary Genres, visit **booklinks.abdopublishing.com**. These links are routinely monitored and updated to provide the most current information available.

FOR MORE INFORMATION

For more information on this subject, contact or visit the following organizations:

Chinese Historical Society of America
965 Clay Street, San Francisco, CA 94108
415-391-1188
http://chsa.org/
San Francisco is home to the oldest and largest Chinatown in the United States. Founded in 1963, the Chinese Historical Society of America features exhibits highlighting the history of the Chinese in America.

Jane Austen's House Museum
Chawton, Alton, Hampshire, GU34 1SD
01420-83262
http://www.jane-austens-house-museum.org.uk/#!contact/c6gz
Jane Austen lived in this home in Hampshire, England, from 1809 until shortly before her death in 1817. Today, the home is furnished much as it may have been when Austen lived there and features many Austen artifacts, including letters, manuscript notes, and editions of her novels.

United States Holocaust Memorial Museum
100 Raoul Wallenberg Place SW, Washington, DC, 20024-2126
202-488-0400
https://www.ushmm.org/
The United States Holocaust Memorial Museum features artifacts, video footage, and photographs relating the atrocities of the Holocaust. A special exhibit focuses on how Germans aided in Hitler's quest to exterminate the Jews but also highlights the stories of those who hid and protected Jewish neighbors and strangers.

SOURCE NOTES

CHAPTER 1. INTRODUCTION TO LITERARY GENRES

None.

CHAPTER 2. AN OVERVIEW OF *PRIDE AND PREJUDICE*

1. Jane Austen. *Pride and Prejudice*. New York: Penguin, 1985. Print. 186.
2. Ibid. 218.

CHAPTER 3. ELIZABETH BENNET AS A STRONG WOMAN

1. Jane Austen. *Pride and Prejudice*. New York: Penguin, 1985. Print. 51.
2. Ibid. 163.
3. Ibid. 51.
4. Ibid. 175.
5. Ibid. 163.
6. Ibid. 165.
7. Ibid. 236.
8. Ibid. 390.

CHAPTER 4. AN OVERVIEW OF *THE BOOK THIEF*

1. Markus Zusak. *The Book Thief*. New York: Knopf, 2005. Print. 74.

CHAPTER 5. WORDS AND MORALITY IN *THE BOOK THIEF*

1. Markus Zusak. *The Book Thief*. New York: Knopf, 2005. Print. 56.
2. Ibid. 262.
3. Ibid. 499.
4. Ibid. 110.
5. Ibid. 147.
6. Ibid. 273.
7. Ibid. 63.
8. Ibid. 254.
9. Ibid. 63.
10. Ibid. 398.
11. Ibid. 254.

CHAPTER 6. AN OVERVIEW OF *THE JOY LUCK CLUB*

1. Amy Tan. *The Joy Luck Club*. New York: Penguin, 1989. Print. 253.
2. Ibid. 247.

CHAPTER 7. STEREOTYPES AND IDENTITY IN *THE JOY LUCK CLUB*

1. Amy Tan. *The Joy Luck Club*. New York: Penguin, 1989. Print. 215.
2. Ibid. 251.
3. Ibid. 263.
4. Ibid. 17.
5. Ibid. 254.
6. Ibid. 259.
7. Ibid. 31.

CHAPTER 8. OVERVIEWS OF *BRAVE NEW WORLD* AND *THE HANDMAID'S TALE*

1. Aldous Huxley. *Brave New World*. New York: HarperPerennial, 1998. Print. 54.
2. Ibid. 67.

CHAPTER 9. POWER AND CONTROL

1. Aldous Huxley. *Brave New World*. New York: HarperPerennial, 1998. Print. 228.
2. Ibid. 148.
3. Margaret Atwood. *The Handmaid's Tale*. New York: Anchor, 1986. Print. 270.
4. Ibid. 286.

INDEX

ABOUT THE AUTHOR

Valerie Bodden has written more than 200 nonfiction books for children. Her books have received positive reviews from *School Library Journal*, *Booklist*, *Children's Literature*, *ForeWord Magazine*, *Horn Book Guide*, *VOYA*, and *Library Media Connection*. Valerie lives in Wisconsin with her husband and four young children.